KT-382-692

This *LADYBIRD TALE*
belongs to

....

Cinderella

Retold by Vera Southgate M.A., B.COM
with illustrations by Yunhee Park

LADYBIRD TALES

ONCE UPON A TIME there was a little girl called Cinderella. Her mother was dead and she lived with her father and two stepsisters.

Cinderella's stepsisters were fair of face but, because they were bad-tempered and unkind, their faces grew to look ugly. They were jealous of Cinderella because she was a lovely child, and so they were often unkind to her.

The stepsisters made Cinderella do all the work in the house. She worked from morning till night without stopping.

Cinderella not only did all the housework but she also helped her stepsisters to dress. She cleaned their shoes, brushed their hair, tied their ribbons and fastened their buckles.

The sisters had many fine clothes, but all Cinderella had was an old dress and a pair of wooden shoes.

After she had worked until she was weary, Cinderella had no bed to go to. She had to sleep by the hearth in the cinders. That was why her stepsisters called her Cinderella and that was why she always looked dusty and dirty.

Now it happened that the king arranged a great feast for his son. The feast was to last three days and on each evening there was to be a grand ball. All the beautiful young girls in the country were invited, in order that the prince might choose himself a bride.

Cinderella's stepsisters were invited to the feast. Cinderella was not invited. Everyone thought that she was her sisters' maid.

On the evening of the first ball, Cinderella had to help her sisters to get dressed. Cinderella thought of how she would like to go to the ball and tears began to run down her face.

"I would like to wear a beautiful dress and go to the ball," said Cinderella.

"A fine sight you would be at a ball!" laughed the stepsisters. When they had left, poor Cinderella sat down and cried. Suddenly, she heard a voice saying, "What is the matter, my dear?" There stood her fairy godmother, smiling kindly at her.

"I would like to go to the ball," said Cinderella.

"And so you shall, my dear," said her fairy godmother. "Dry your eyes and then do exactly as I tell you."

"First, go into the garden and bring me the biggest pumpkin you can find," said the fairy godmother.

"Very well," said Cinderella and she ran off to the garden. She picked the biggest pumpkin she could find and took it to her fairy godmother.

The fairy godmother touched the pumpkin with her magic wand. Immediately, it turned into the most wonderful golden carriage you can imagine. The inside was lined with red velvet.

"Now run and fetch me the mousetrap from the pantry," said the fairy godmother.

Cinderella ran off to the pantry. She found the mousetrap on the floor. There were six mice in it.

Cinderella brought the mousetrap to her fairy godmother. One touch of the magic wand and the mice turned into six fine grey horses.

"Next, fetch me the rat trap from the cellar," said the fairy godmother.

Cinderella ran down the steps to the cellar. She found the rat trap, with one rat in it, and took it to her fairy godmother.

One touch of the fairy wand and the rat changed into a smart coachman, dressed in red livery trimmed with gold braid.

"Lastly," said Cinderella's fairy godmother, "I want you to bring me the two lizards that are behind the cucumber frame at the bottom of the garden."

Cinderella ran into the garden and there she found two small lizards.

Cinderella's fairy godmother touched the lizards with her fairy wand. They turned into two smart footmen.

There was now a golden coach, lined with red velvet, drawn by six grey horses. There was a coachman, in red livery, to drive the coach, and two fine footmen to open the doors.

Cinderella glanced down at her old, tattered dress and her wooden shoes. "One more touch of my magic wand, my dear," said her fairy godmother. Then there happened the most wonderful magic of all.

Cinderella found herself in a beautiful ball-gown of pale pink silk. On her feet were dainty pink slippers. Cinderella's face was shining with joy. "Oh! Thank you!" she cried.

"Enjoy yourself at the ball, my dear," said her fairy godmother. "But remember, you must be home before the clock strikes midnight. For, on the last stroke of twelve, all will be as it was before and yourself the ragged girl you were."

The footman opened the door of the carriage. Cinderella sat down on the red velvet cushions. Then they were off.

When Cinderella arrived at the palace, she looked so beautiful that her sisters did not know her.

The prince thought that he had never seen such a beautiful princess. He took her hand and danced with her all evening.
He never let her out of his sight.

Cinderella had never spent such a wonderful evening in her whole life. Yet she still remembered her fairy godmother's warning.

At a quarter to twelve, Cinderella left the ballroom while the other guests were still dancing. Her carriage was waiting for her and she was driven quickly home. She arrived at the door just as the clock was striking twelve.

On the last stroke of midnight, the coach became a pumpkin, the horses became mice, the coachman a rat, and the footmen lizards. Cinderella's ball-gown vanished and she found herself once more in her old grey dress and wooden shoes.

When her stepsisters returned home they could talk about nothing but the beautiful princess at the ball. Cinderella listened but said nothing.

On the second evening, the stepsisters went off to the ball, leaving Cinderella sitting by the fire.

No sooner had they gone than Cinderella's fairy godmother appeared again. Just as before, her magic wand produced the golden carriage with its coachman and footmen.

This time Cinderella's ball-gown was even more beautiful than on the first evening. It was made of pale blue satin, with floating overskirts of pale blue net, embroidered with silver thread. Her pale blue slippers were embroidered in silver.

Once more, Cinderella's fairy godmother reminded her to be home by midnight.

When Cinderella arrived at the ball in her blue dress, everyone was astonished at her beauty. The prince had waited for her and he instantly took her by the hand. As before, he danced with no one but her.

Cinderella was so happy that she almost forgot what her fairy godmother had told her. Suddenly, it was five minutes to twelve. She left the prince and hurried out of the ballroom as quickly as she could.

Cinderella's carriage was waiting. But they were only halfway home when the clock began to strike twelve.

On the last stroke of midnight, Cinderella found herself in her old grey dress and wooden shoes in the middle of a dark, lonely road.

She had to run the rest of the way home, as fast as she could. Even so, she had just seated herself on her stool by the cinders, when her sisters returned from the ball.

Once more, all the stepsisters could talk about was the beautiful stranger with whom the prince had danced.

On the evening of the third ball, Cinderella's fairy godmother appeared as soon the stepsisters had left.

When her fairy godmother touched her with the magic wand, Cinderella found herself in the most splendid and magnificent gown. It was made of silver and gold lace. On her feet were sparkling glass slippers.

Cinderella was so delighted that she hardly knew how to thank her fairy godmother.

"Enjoy yourself, my dear," said her fairy godmother, "but do not forget the time."

When Cinderella arrived at the ball in her dress of silver and gold, she looked so magnificent that everyone was speechless with astonishment.

The prince danced with no one but Cinderella all evening. Cinderella was so happy that she forgot all about the time.

Suddenly, the clock began to strike twelve. Cinderella rushed out of the door in such haste that she lost one of her slippers.

The prince ran after her and saw the slipper. He picked it up. It was small and dainty and made entirely of glass.

By the time Cinderella reached the place where her carriage had been, it had disappeared and she was in her old clothes. This time she had to run all the way home.

The prince looked everywhere for her, but could not find her. He still did not know her name, but he had fallen in love with her and he was determined to marry her.

So, the next morning, the prince took the glass slipper to the king, and said, "No one shall be my wife but she whose foot will fit this glass slipper."

The king's herald was sent through the streets of the city, carrying the small glass slipper on a blue cushion. The prince himself followed, hoping to find the lady with whom he had danced.

Every lady who had been to the feast was eager to try on the slipper. Each one hoped that the slipper would fit her and that she would marry the prince. Many ladies tried to squeeze their feet into the slipper, but their feet were too large for such a dainty shoe.

At last, the herald, followed by the prince, came to Cinderella's house.

Each of the stepsisters was determined to squeeze her foot into the tiny slipper, so that she could marry the prince. But they both had large, ugly feet. Even though they struggled, neither one could force her foot into the slipper.

At last, the prince turned to Cinderella's father and asked, "Have you no other daughter?"

"I have one more," replied the father. Then the stepsisters cried out, "She is much too dirty. She cannot show herself."

But the prince insisted and so Cinderella was sent for.

Cinderella seated herself on her stool, drew her foot out of her heavy wooden shoe, and put it into the slipper, which fitted like a glove.

When Cinderella stood up and the prince looked at her face, he cried out, "This is my true bride."

At that moment, Cinderella's fairy godmother appeared and turned her once more into the beautiful princess. The old grey dress became a velvet gown.

The prince lifted Cinderella onto his horse and rode away with her.

The stepsisters were horrified to discover that Cinderella was the beautiful princess who had been at the three balls. They were so angry that they were pale with rage.

At the palace, the king arranged a magnificent wedding for the prince and Cinderella. All the kings and queens and princes and princesses in the land came to the wedding. The wedding feast lasted a whole week.

And so Cinderella and the prince lived happily ever after.

A History of Cinderella

One of the most popular fairy tales, *Cinderella* has inspired countless picture books, ballets, musicals, operas, films, books and songs.

There are many variations of the story, but the theme of an unlucky girl whose fortune changes can be found in all of them.

The earliest recorded version, by Chinese author and scholar Tuan Ch'eng-shih, was entitled *Ye Xian*. Today's popular retelling is based on Charles Perrault's 1697 version called *Cendrillon, ou la Petite Pantoufle de Verre* (*Cinderella, or the Little Glass Slipper*).

The Brothers Grimm included the story in their collection of tales published 1812-1815. This version has the fairy godmother turning the pumpkin into a carriage and animals into footmen.

Ladybird's classic 1964 edition, retold by Vera Southgate, has delighted thousands of children, reinforcing its popularity today.

Collect more fantastic

LADYBIRD  TALES

9781409311072

9781409311119

9781409311102

9781409311126

The Gingerbread Man

9781409311096

The Three Little Pigs

9781409311089

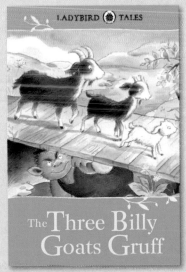

The Three Billy Goats Gruff

9781409311065

Hansel and Gretel

9781409311133

Endpapers taken from series 606d,
first published in 1964

A catalogue record for this book is available from the British Library

Published by Ladybird Books Ltd
80 Strand London WC2R 0RL
A Penguin Company

007

© Ladybird Books Ltd MMXII

ISBN: 978-1-40931-107-2

Printed in China